Animals in the City

Written by Jo Windsor

Rigby

This is a city.

Some animals
live in a city.

PORT OF SAN FRANCISCO

These monkeys
don't live
in the city.

This cat does live in the city.

This bird does live in the city, too.

This rat does
live in the city.

Foxes don't live in the city.

Bears don't live in the city.

Look at the animals.

Which animals live in the city?

Index

Guide Notes

Title: Animals in the City
Stage: Early (1) – Red

Genre: Nonfiction
Approach: Guided Reading
Processes: Thinking Critically, Exploring Language, Processing Information
Written and Visual Focus: Photographs (static images), Index
Word Count: 61

THINKING CRITICALLY

(sample questions)
- What do you think this book is going to tell us?
- Look at the title and read it to the children.
- Ask the children what they know about animals that live in the city.
- Focus the children's attention on the index. Ask: "What are you going to find out about in this book?"
- Where do you think there might be some places in the world where bears and foxes and monkeys DO live in the city?
- Why do you think a bird would live in the city?
- Where do you think a rat would live in the city?

EXPLORING LANGUAGE

Terminology
Title, cover, photographs, author, photographers

Vocabulary
Interest words: city, animals, live, monkeys, cat, bird, rat, fox, bear, food
High-frequency word (reinforced): too
Positional word: in

Print Conventions
Capital letter for sentence beginnings, periods, comma, question mark